THE COMPUTER CAPER

CHRISTOPHER CLARO

Illustrations by John Hatzakis

Copyright © 1989 by Scholastic Inc.
All rights reserved. Published by Scholastic Inc.
SPRINT and SPRINT BOOKS are trademarks of Scholastic Inc.
Printed in the U.S.A.
ISBN 0-590-35203-2

10   31   03 02 01 00

CHAPTER 1

BETWEEN OUR OLD FRIENDS JEFFERSON AND MONROE, THERE LIES A NAME THAT CAN BE OF HELP TO YOU.

Bonnie Madigan stared at the strange message on her computer screen. She had been trying to contact her friend Crew when it appeared.

Instead of talking on the phone, Bonnie and Crew communicated with their computers. They typed messages into their computers, and the computers sent and received signals over the telephone lines.

Now that Bonnie had this message on her screen, she couldn't use her computer to send a message to Crew. She went downstairs to the kitchen and dialed his number on the phone.

Her father was preparing his lunch in the kitchen. "Are you really going to talk on the telephone?" he asked.

"Yes," Bonnie answered. "I got a really weird message on my computer."

"What kind of message?" her father asked.

"It's something about Presidents," Bonnie said. "I'm calling Crew to see if he sent it."

As she waited for Crew to answer, flashes of lightning lit up the kitchen, followed by sharp claps of thunder.

"You know," Mr. Madigan said, "this is quite a storm we're having. It could have something to do with your weird message. Bad weather sometimes causes problems with the phone lines."

"Hello, Mrs. Van Berg," Bonnie said. "May I speak with Crew, please?"

"Oh, hello, Bonnie," said Mrs. Van Berg. "It's so odd to hear your voice over the telephone."

"Yes, I know," Bonnie said. "I can't get through

5

to Crew's computer. I think it's because of the storm."

"Well, just hold on a moment," Mrs. Van Berg said. "I'll call Townshend to the phone."

Bonnie smiled when she heard Crew's mother use his real name. Then Crew picked up the phone.

"Hi, Bonnie."

"Hey, how's it going, Townshend?" Bonnie knew she could annoy Crew by calling him by his real name. He didn't like his name at all. He had gotten his nickname when he started wearing his hair in a crewcut.

"First of all," Crew said, "don't call me that."

"And second?" Bonnie asked.

"Hold on for a minute, while I check something."

Crew put the phone down for a few seconds. When he came back, he had a question for Bonnie. "Did you know that this is only the third time this year that you and I have talked on the phone?"

"The first time was during that blizzard last winter," Bonnie said.

"And the second time," Crew said, "was when you called to tell me to watch that show about robots on TV."

"Well, this time," Bonnie said, "I'm calling to tell you about a really strange message that is on my screen."

6

She told him what the message said. He was as curious as she was. "I'll be over as soon as the rain stops," Crew said.

After the storm passed, Crew hopped on his bike and rode the mile to Bonnie's house. He was always trying to beat his own time on that one-mile stretch.

"My best time," he told her as he walked into the house.

"How long?" Bonnie asked.

"Three minutes, thirty-five seconds."

"Pretty good," Bonnie said, smiling.

"Well, aren't you going to ask me what route I took?" Crew asked.

Bonnie didn't really care. But she asked anyway. "What route did you take?"

"I cut across the parking lot at the mall," Crew said. "And then I went down the alley next to the bakery."

"The whole town is proud of you," Bonnie said. "But we have other things to discuss. Come upstairs and take a look at the message on my screen."

As they headed for the stairs, Mr. Madigan came out of the kitchen.

"Hi, Crew," he said. "Did you make good time?"

"Three thirty-five," Crew said proudly.

"Oh, really?" Mr. Madigan said. "What route did you take?"

"I cut across the parking lot at the mall — "

Bonnie went ahead without Crew. She wanted to see whether the message was still on her computer screen.

After a minute Crew joined her. "How come your dad is at home?" Crew asked as he walked into Bonnie's room.

"He's on vacation," Bonnie answered. Then she pointed to the computer screen in front of her. "Look at this," she said.

He read the message aloud. "Between our old friends Jefferson and Monroe, there lies a name that can be of help to you. Hmmm."

"It looks as if we have a little research to do," Bonnie said. "I've already saved this message on a disk. It took quite a while, so I think this screenful is just the beginning of a long program."

"Smart move," Crew said. "The message might have gotten here because the storm messed up the phone lines. If so, it will disappear when the lines are fixed."

"That's what I figured," said Bonnie. "Now, let's find out who was President between Jefferson and Monroe."

They went downstairs. Mr. Madigan was sitting at the kitchen table reading a book.

"Dad," Bonnie said, "do you know who was President between Thomas Jefferson and James Monroe?"

"No," Mr. Madigan said. "But we have an encyclopedia that cost me a lot of money. And I'm sure it has the answer to your question."

Bonnie went to the living room and pulled out the "P" volume of the encyclopedia. She turned to the "Presidents" section.

"Let's see, now," Bonnie said. She ran her

finger down the page. "OK. Here's Thomas Jefferson."

Crew looked over Bonnie's shoulder. "And right after him comes James Madison."

"Let's try it," Bonnie said. She put the book back and ran upstairs. Crew followed.

Bonnie typed "James Madison" into the computer. The screen blinked a few times.

When it stopped blinking, a new message was on the screen.

COME ON, PALS! REMEMBER THE OLD DAYS!

"Now, what does that mean?" Bonnie asked.

"I have no idea," Crew said.

They stared at the screen in silence. Then they heard Mr. Madigan's voice from the bottom of the stairs. "Bonnie!" he called.

Bonnie didn't get up from her chair. "Yes, Dad," she yelled.

"Do you think you could come to the head of the stairs? So I don't have to shout?"

Bonnie got up and went to the stairs. "Sorry, Dad," she said.

Mr. Madigan said, "Your mother wants you to take some things to the dry cleaner's this afternoon. She left them in the hall."

"OK, Dad," Bonnie said. Then she went back to her room. "I've got an errand to do for Mom. Shall we go do it now?" she said to Crew.

"Yeah," Crew said. "We aren't getting anywhere with this."

Bonnie took the disk out and turned off the computer. She and Crew went downstairs and picked up the clothes. Then they headed out to their bikes. As they rode to the dry cleaner's, they talked about the message.

"What do you think it meant?" Crew asked.

"I don't know," Bonnie said. "It looked like a clue for a treasure hunt."

"Maybe it's a joke or something," Crew said.

"You might be right," Bonnie said as they pulled up to the dry cleaner's. She got off her bike and went in.

"I'm staying out here," Crew called after her.
"I'm going to practice my wheelies."

Crew pulled his front wheel high in the air
and rode for about a block. He had gone back
and forth three times when he stopped to rest.
Sitting on his bike, he looked up at the street
sign. Then his face lit up. He rode back to the
dry cleaner's. Bonnie was walking out just as he
pulled up.

"Bonnie, come with me!" Crew said. "I've

got something very interesting to show you."

"What is it?" Bonnie asked.

"Just follow me!" he said.

Bonnie got on her bike and followed him for a block. They stopped in front of a coffee shop.

"What is this place?" Crew asked her.

Bonnie looked at him as if she thought he was crazy.

"This is a coffee shop," she said. "People on our planet sometimes eat their meals here."

"No, no, no!" Crew said. "The name of the place!"

Bonnie looked up and read the sign out loud: "Monroe's Coffee Shop." She looked at Crew. Now she was taking him seriously.

"Right," Crew said. "Now go look at the street sign on the corner."

Bonnie rode to the corner. When she got there, she looked at the sign. She yelled back to Crew, "Jefferson Street!"

"And what's between them?" Crew yelled.

Between the street sign and the coffee shop stood the Carver City Savings Bank. Crew and Bonnie rode back to her house as fast as they could.

They charged into the house. Bonnie took the stairs up to her room two at a time. Crew was right behind her.

She put the disk into the computer and waited for the program to load. The screen blinked and the message came up again.

BETWEEN OUR OLD FRIENDS JEFFERSON AND MONROE, THERE LIES A NAME THAT CAN BE OF HELP TO YOU.

Bonnie typed in "Carver City Savings Bank." The screen blinked for a few seconds and then flashed:

VERY GOOD! HERE'S MORE . . .

CHAPTER 2

OK, FRIENDS, REMEMBER ALL THOSE
GREAT FISHING TRIPS WE USED TO
TAKE? WELL, HEAD ON OVER TO
NEMO'S FISHING SUPPLY. CATALOG
NUMBER L511 WILL HELP YOU TACKLE
ANOTHER CLUE.

"L511?" Bonnie said. "What could that mean?"

"Let's see what we have to work with," Crew said. "A bank and a store that sells fishing supplies."

"Right," Bonnie said. "The treasure that we're looking for must be either money or worms."

Crew laughed. Then, as they walked toward their bikes, Crew tried to put the clues together. "Maybe it has something to do with fishing from the bank of a river," he said.

"Could be," Bonnie said, with a smile. "Let's get down to Nemo's and find out what L511 means. Maybe that will help."

Nemo's tackle shop was a huge store. "Look at the size of this place," Crew said as they walked in.

"Yeah," Bonnie said. "I never knew you needed this much equipment just to catch fish."

"Sure," said Crew, picking something off a display rack. "You wouldn't want to leave without this. It's a special jackknife. It has over a hundred different uses."

"You study all its uses," Bonnie said. "I'm going to find out about this L511."

She walked up to a counter where another customer was waiting. The store owner was on top of a ladder. He was wearing a ship captain's hat and a shirt covered with pictures of jumping fish. "Excuse me, please," Bonnie said. "I need a little information about something in your catalog."

"I'll be right with you, miss," the man said.

"Bucky," he called, "where did you put the rubber worms?"

"Which ones?" Bucky's voice was coming from the bottom of the basement stairs.

"The ones that just came in."

Bucky came up out of the basement. "They're right near the new flies, Captain. The ones that glow in the dark."

The Captain climbed down the ladder. "Well, I can't find them," he said. "This man would like twelve of them." The customer seemed very tired of waiting for the worms.

The Captain turned to Bonnie. "Well now, what can Captain Nemo do for you, dear?"

"I'd like to see number L511 in your catalog," Bonnie told him.

"L511?" The Captain thought for a few seconds. "Hmmm . . . that would be a tackle box. Bucky!" he called. "Can you get me an L511 tackle box?"

Bonnie figured it would take a long time. She wandered over to where Crew was. He was still looking at the knife.

"This is the greatest knife!" Crew said. "Look at what it has in it: a fish cleaner, a bottle opener, even a scissors!" Just then Bonnie heard the Captain's voice.

"Here it is, little missy," he said. "The L511. It's the finest tackle box we sell."

Crew and Bonnie looked closely at the tackle box. The captain told them about it.

"Yes sir-ee, the finest tackle box we sell," he said. "It's the Safe and Sound Bait Vault."

"Bait vault?" Crew said. "I always thought a bucket was a safe enough place for bait."

"Oh, you'd be surprised, young fellow," the Captain said. "Some bait is mighty expensive. People like to protect their belongings."

"How much is this box?" Bonnie asked as she picked it up off the counter. It was made of shiny blue metal. It had a lock on the front.

"It's $125," the Captain said.

"Oh," Bonnie said. "That's a little more than we can afford. But thank you anyway."

She started to walk out of the store. Crew wanted to stay. "I haven't finished looking at the knife," he said. "I haven't seen all the uses."

But Bonnie was on her way out the door. Crew put the knife back on the rack. He mumbled, "I'll have to come back. That's some knife!"

As Crew left, the Captain called, "Bucky! You can put the bait vault back downstairs."

Bucky came over and took the tackle box off the counter. "That's funny," he said to the Captain. "There were two guys in here this morning who wanted to see an L511."

The Captain wasn't paying attention. "It's the finest tackle box we sell."

On the ride home, Bonnie complained about the way the Captain had talked to her. "I hate it when people who don't even know me call me 'dear' or 'darling.'"

"Or 'little missy'?" Crew said.

"Now, there's one I *really* hate!" Bonnie said.

Crew changed the subject. "What do you think the tackle box means?" he asked.

"I don't know," she said. "Maybe it has nothing to do with fish, or bait. Maybe the clue is the word 'tackle.'"

Crew looked doubtful. "But what could 'tackle' mean?"

"I don't know," Bonnie said again. "But we aren't giving up yet. Let's tell the computer about the Safe and Sound Bait Vault. Then we'll see if it will give us another clue."

In a few minutes they were back in Bonnie's room. Bonnie sat down in front of the computer and typed "Safe and Sound Bait Vault."

The computer blinked. Then it answered:
VERY GOOD, CHUMS! HERE'S MORE!

CHAPTER 3

NOW, IT'S ON TO THE COMMUNITY CENTER. BUT YOU WON'T BE PLAYING CHECKERS. YOU'RE GOING TO BE ART CRITICS! EXAMINE A PAINTING. TO FIGURE OUT WHICH ONE IT IS, THINK OF SNOW WHITE'S LITTLE FRIENDS. THEN SUBTRACT TWO. THEN THINK OF THE SUNSET. IF YOU'RE WATCHING IT, THE PAINTING WILL BE ON YOUR RIGHT.

"All right," Bonnie said. "Let's figure out what we have here."

"Well, there's this part about Snow White."

"OK," Bonnie said. "Her little friends are the seven dwarfs."

"Right. And if you subtract two, you have five."

"Yes. Now what about the sunset?" Bonnie asked.

"The sun rises in the east," Crew said.

"And it sets in the west."

"I guess the next thing to do," Crew said, "is to get on over to the Community Center."

They got on their bikes and started the ride to the Community Center.

"How about a shortcut?" Crew asked.

"I don't know," Bonnie said. "I think we should stick to the main roads on this trip. We'll use a shortcut next time. I promise."

"All right," Crew said. "I'll remember that."

Soon they were standing inside the door of the Community Center, trying to figure out which way was west.

"You know," Crew said, "this would have been a lot easier if I had bought that knife. It also had a compass in it."

Bonnie ignored him. "It's past noon," she said, "so the sun should be west of us."

Bonnie and Crew looked out a large window. They could see the sun shining through the top branches of some trees.

"We're facing west," Bonnie said. "So we should turn to the right."

They turned to the right and looked at the wall. It was covered with paintings.

"OK," Bonnie said. "The clue is in one of those paintings. And it has something to do with the number 5."

She counted the paintings from the door. The fifth one was not very helpful. It was made up of blotches of paint splattered on the canvas.

Meanwhile, Crew was looking at the other end of the wall. "Hey," he called. "Take a look at this."

Bonnie walked over to where Crew was standing. He was looking at a painting of the Carver City Bus Station.

"What are you thinking?" she asked.

"What's in front of the bus station?" Crew asked.

"A bus," Bonnie said.

"And what number is on the bus?" Crew asked.

"Number five," Bonnie said. Then she smiled.

"A painting of the bus station," she said, as they left the building. "Maybe it means that whatever we're looking for is out of town."

"Or maybe the clue is the number five," Crew said. "Let's find out what the computer has to say about this."

When they got back to Bonnie's house, Mr. Madigan was fixing a broken window in the garage door.

"Hi, Dad," said Bonnie, as she and Crew rode up.

"Hi, Mr. M.," Crew said.

"Back again?" said Mr. Madigan. "Didn't you two just leave?"

Bonnie smiled. "We'll explain later, Dad. Right now, we're sort of in a hurry."

Mr. Madigan shrugged and went back to work. Bonnie and Crew ran up to Bonnie's room. Bonnie flipped the switch on the computer and loaded the program. The clue about the Community Center came up.

"Let's try 'five,'" Crew said.

Bonnie typed "five" on the keyboard. The screen blinked, but didn't respond.

"Hey, I've got an idea!" Bonnie said. She typed in "Carver City Bus Station."

The screen blinked. Then a new message appeared.

YOU'RE GETTING GOOD! I THINK YOU
DESERVE ANOTHER CLUE.

CHAPTER 4

OK, FRIENDS. LET'S GET ROLLING.
SKATE OVER TO THE ? TO UNLOCK
MORE MYSTERIES.

"Skate over to the question mark?" Bonnie said. "What could that mean?"

"I think I know," Crew said. "It probably means that old roller skating rink, the Skate Key. But that place has been closed for a long time."

"Now what could we possibly find at the Skate Key?" Bonnie said. "There's nothing there except weeds and an empty parking lot."

"Well, there must be something," Crew said. "And it's a long ride. So we'd better get going."

Crew figured it would be a thirty-minute ride from Bonnie's house to the Skate Key if they used his best shortcuts.

"Can't we just stick to the main roads?" Bonnie asked. They were riding through an empty lot where the ground was covered with broken bottles.

"You don't realize how much time we're saving," Crew said.

"You're right, Crew. If we hadn't gone this way, it might have taken an extra ten minutes. And we wouldn't have had all this fun dodging broken glass."

Their trip ended with a ride across an old baseball field. It brought them to a hill that overlooked the Skate Key.

"I didn't think you were going to make it," Crew said.

"I'm used to riding on pavement," Bonnie said. She was a little bit annoyed. "Now, let's get down there."

"Hey, wait a minute," Crew said. He was looking down at the parking lot. "There are two guys down there."

"Where?"

"Right down there." Crew pointed to the parking lot. Sure enough, there were two men walking around the entrance to the rink.

"What do you think they're doing?" Bonnie asked.

"I'd say they were looking for something," Crew said.

The men were walking slowly around the

building. They were trying to look through the windows, which were boarded up.

"Let's stay up here for a little while," Crew said.

After a few minutes, the two men stopped looking. They leaned on the hood of a green car. One of them wore a red shirt. They were talking to each other. The one with the red shirt seemed much more excited than the other one.

"That guy looks as if he's having a fit," Bonnie said. The man was waving his arms and slamming his fist on the hood of the car.

"Something down there must have really upset him," Crew said. "I can't wait to get down there and find out what it is."

Finally the two men got into the car. The man with the red shirt got in on the driver's side. For a minute the car didn't move. Then it started to roll through the parking lot toward the street.

Crew got on his bike and got ready to ride down the hill. "Wait a minute," Bonnie said. "Let's wait till they're out of sight."

The car made a lot of noise on its way out. Bonnie watched it until it disappeared in the distance. "OK, let's go," she said.

Crew backed his bicycle up a little bit before he went down the hill. Then he cried, "Here goes!" He let out a loud "Wheeeee!" as he went down the hill at top speed. Bonnie took it a little more slowly.

Crew left a long skid mark on the pavement as he came to a stop in the parking lot. He started circling the rink slowly on his bike. Bonnie followed behind him.

"What could we be looking for?" Bonnie called to Crew.

"Well," Crew said, "let's put all the clues together. We have the bank."

"Right," said Bonnie. "And the tackle box."

"Yeah," Crew said. "And the painting."

"Where does that leave us?" Bonnie asked.

The two of them stopped at the back of the

rink. Crew said, "I don't know. It beats me."

They rode around to the front of the building. The sign over the front entrance said: "The Skat Key, 1284 Longwood Road, Carver City." Bonnie looked at the space where the "e" had fallen off the word "skate."

"Maybe that missing 'e' can tell us something," she said.

They got off their bikes and sat down on the ground. There were weeds growing out of cracks in the parking lot. The paint on the building was peeling. Bonnie was getting uncomfortable.

"This place is a little creepy," she said. "It's

so quiet. I don't think we should hang around."

"Yeah," Crew said. "Let's get out of here."

"All right. But this time we'll take my route," Bonnie said.

Bonnie's route took an extra ten minutes. "I don't care," she told Crew. "At least there's no broken glass."

As soon as they got back to Bonnie's house, they went straight to her computer.

"Well, we might as well try the simplest answer first," Bonnie said. She typed in: "Skate Key."

The screen blinked, but didn't respond.

31

"Wait," Crew said. "I just thought of something. Try 'Skat Key' — you know, 'skate' without the 'e.'"

Bonnie typed in "Skat Key."

The computer answered:

BRILLIANT, BROTHERS! WHAT IS THE ADDRESS?

Crew stopped and looked at the screen. "That's all it wants to know?" he asked. "Just the address?"

Bonnie typed:

1284 LONGWOOD

The computer responded:

WELL DONE! I HOPE THE CLUES ARE STARTING TO FALL INTO PLACE. HERE COMES THE LAST ONE.

Crew and Bonnie stared at the computer screen.

IT'S TIME TO MAKE A VISIT TO THE CARVER CITY CEMETERY. SEE THE TOMBSTONE OF MAJOR PARRISH. TRY 4:00.

"Oh, boy!" Crew said. "Now things are really getting weird."

Bonnie looked at her watch. It was already after six o'clock. "It's too late to go today," she said.

"Tomorrow afternoon," Crew said. "We have a date with a dead major."

CHAPTER 5

Crew met Bonnie the next afternoon. She had been doing some research.

"Major Parrish was a World War II fighter pilot," she told Crew. "And he was a great hero. He won a lot of medals for his bravery. After he retired, he lived here in Carver City."

"And now we have to go check out his grave," Crew said. "What time is it?"

"It's three-thirty," Bonnie said. "We want to make it to the cemetery before four o'clock. We'd better get going."

As they rode, Bonnie began getting a little nervous. "I've never liked graveyards," she said.

"You thought the Skate Key was creepy," Crew said. "Wait till you've spent a few minutes in the cemetery."

"Thanks," Bonnie said. "Thanks a lot. You're really making me feel better."

The back entrance to the cemetery was at the end of a deserted road. There were no houses on it. The only sound Crew and Bonnie could hear was the wind blowing through the trees.

Crew broke the silence. "I saw this movie once where some people were driving past a cemetery at night and — "

"I don't want to hear about it, thank you very much," Bonnie said.

"Oh. OK," Crew said.

When they got to the entrance, they stopped

their bikes and looked around. There were no other people in sight. The wind made an eerie noise. Now even Crew was getting a little nervous.

"Well," he said, "what are we waiting for? Let's go find the Major's grave."

A dirt path snaked its way through the graveyard. They walked their bikes along it carefully. They passed row after row of tombstones.

"Let's talk about something," Bonnie said.

"Like what?" Crew asked.

"I don't know. How about English grammar?"

"You mean I before E, except after C, and all that?" Crew asked.

"That's spelling," Bonnie said. Her voice was quivering. "I just want something to take our minds off the fact that we're surrounded by dead people," she continued.

"Let's try a spelling bee," Crew said.

"OK. You give me one, and I'll give you one."

"All right," Crew said. "Spell *terrified*."

"B-O-N-N-I-E," she said, giggling.

"That's good," Crew said. Then he pointed to something up ahead. "Look! I think we've found the Major's tombstone."

He was right. The grave was beside a paved

MAJOR ROBERT "ACES HIGH" PARRISH

1908 - 1979

road that led to the main entrance of the cemetery. The Major's tombstone was bigger than most of the others. There was a statue of the Major above the tombstone. His name and dates were carved on the base of the statue: "Major Robert 'Aces High' Parrish, 1908-1979."

Bonnie looked at her watch. "It's five minutes to four," she said.

"OK," Crew said. "Let's just sit and wait."

Five minutes later, Crew and Bonnie heard a church bell chime four o'clock. Bonnie got a little more nervous.

"You think something is going to jump out of the grave?" Crew asked. She didn't answer him.

They sat for five more minutes. Still nothing happened. All of a sudden, Crew stood up. He started walking slowly around the statue.

"I can't believe I missed this," he said. "It's so obvious."

Bonnie looked at Crew. "What's obvious?"

"'Four o'clock' doesn't mean the time," Crew said. "'Four o'clock' is a position!"

"Take it easy," Bonnie said. "I think this place is getting to you more than you realize."

"No, listen. The base of the statue is a circle," Crew said. "It's just like a clock. I'm walking around to the four o'clock position on the base. It's a system that airplane pilots use when they want to tell where an object is located in the sky."

At the four o'clock position on the base, there was a small model airplane made of steel. Crew leaned down and looked closely at the plane. He saw something underneath one of the wings. It was a key, and it was fastened to the wing with a magnet. Crew pulled it off the magnet.

"Bingo!" he said. He walked over to Bonnie

and held the key out for her to see.

Bonnie took the key from him and looked at it.

"What do you think it's for?" she asked.

"I can think of one thing," Crew said. "It might open the tackle box."

"Then let's get over to Nemo's," Bonnie said.

They hopped on their bikes and rode back along the dirt path. Seconds later, a green car came driving up the paved road. It stopped at Major Parrish's tombstone. Two men got out of the car. They were the same two men that Crew and Bonnie had seen at the roller rink.

"This is the place, Phil," one man said.

The other man looked at his watch. "We're late, Harry," he said. "We're ten minutes late."

Harry rolled his eyes. "Phil, what did I tell you? Didn't I just finish saying that four o'clock was a position and not a time?"

"Yeah, sure," said Phil. He looked at his watch again. "Now we're eleven minutes late."

"I give up," said Harry, waving his arm at Phil. Harry walked around the base of the statue to the four o'clock position. Seeing the model airplane, he ran his hands over and under the wings. He felt the magnet and pulled it off the wing.

"Ah hah!" he exclaimed. "I think we have something here!"

Phil looked at the object in Harry's hand. "Yeah, we have a magnet. So what?"

"So," Harry said, "there must have been something attached to this magnet. And somebody must have gotten to it before we did."

"Yeah," said Phil. "Somebody who was here at four o'clock."

Harry groaned.

"So what do you think was stuck to the magnet?" asked Phil.

"I don't know," said Harry. "Let's go over the clues: There's the bank, the tackle box, the bus station, and the skate key — of course! That's it!"

"What's it?" asked Phil.

"A key was stuck to that magnet!" said Harry. "That's what the clue about the Skate Key meant!"

"But why would we want a skate key?" asked Phil.

"We *don't* want a skate key," yelled Harry. "I'm talking about a real key! A real key that could help us get that $250,000!"

"But it looks as if someone else knew the key was here," Phil said. "I knew there would be trouble with those dopey computer clues."

"Well, Natwick doesn't trust the mail or the phones in jail," said Harry. "He thought the computer would be the safest way to tell us where the money is."

"Yeah," complained Phil. "It's so safe that now somebody else has our key!"

"Hey," Harry said. "Didn't you see some kids on bicycles when we first drove up?"

"Yeah," said Phil. "They went down that dirt path over there."

"We've got to figure out where those kids went," said Harry. "Now let me think . . . the clue before the skate key clue was the one about the bus station — "

They looked at each other. "We'd better get over to the bus station," Phil said.

They got in the car and drove back along the paved road toward the front entrance of the cemetery.

Meanwhile, Crew and Bonnie were well on their way to Nemo's. "If this key fits in the L511," Crew said, "we may solve this mystery."

"Right," Bonnie said. "All these clues might just fall into place."

Bonnie and Crew burst into Nemo's and walked straight to the counter. When the Captain saw Bonnie, he called to the stockboy: "Bucky! An L511!"

Bonnie smiled at the Captain. The Captain, though, didn't seem too happy to see her again.

Bucky brought the tackle box up and placed it in front of Bonnie. Crew took the key out of his pocket and tried it in the lock. It didn't fit.

Crew and Bonnie looked at each other, disappointed. As they left, the Captain called after them, "Come back soon. We get a real kick out of showing that tackle box."

"Well," said Crew, leaning on his bike, "what do we do now?"

"I have an idea," Bonnie said. "We have that painting of the bus station, right?"

"Right," Crew said.

"And we have the number '1284,' from the Skate Key address, right?"

"Right," Crew repeated.

"Well," Bonnie said, "what if '1284' is a route number at the bus station?"

"Route number?" Crew said. "What do you mean?"

"You know," Bonnie said. "Like at the airport. 'Flight 1284 now boarding for Cleveland.'"

"Well," Crew said, "it's too late to go now."

"Right," Bonnie agreed. "First thing in the morning we'll go."

"I'll meet you there at nine," he said.

On the other side of town, Phil and Harry pulled up in front of the bus station. "We don't even know what the kids look like," Harry said. "I didn't get a good look at them. Did you?"

"No," Phil said. "But we'll know who they are."

"How?" asked Harry.

"They'll be the kids with our key," said Phil.

Harry groaned.

CHAPTER 6

The next morning, Crew got to the bus station first. As he stood near the door, waiting for Bonnie, he studied the key closely. It looked as if something had been engraved in the metal. But he couldn't make out what it was.

As soon as Bonnie arrived, Crew said, "Look at this. I think there was something written on this key."

"Well," Bonnie said, "good morning to you too."

"I think it might have been a name," Crew said. "Or a number. Or something."

"Let's deal with that later," Bonnie said. "First we have to find bus route 1284."

Bonnie and Crew walked into the bus station. They stopped when they saw an overhead television screen. The screen displayed information for bus passengers. It showed what time the buses left, what cities they went to, and what the route numbers were.

"Oh, no!" Bonnie said. "These route numbers have only three numbers in them. '1284' has four numbers."

"We'll have to think of something else," Crew said.

"I'm out of ideas," Bonnie said. "I think we may have to give up."

Just then they saw a woman carrying two babies. She was struggling to put some luggage into a locker while holding both babies.

"Let's give her a hand," Bonnie said.

"Might as well," Crew said.

"Excuse me," Bonnie said to the woman. "Can we help you?"

"That would be wonderful," the woman said.

She handed one baby to Crew. Then she handed the other to Bonnie. As they held the children, the woman pushed a suitcase into a locker. Bonnie was staring at the locker.

"Hey," she said to Crew.

Crew was bouncing his baby up and down in his arms. "Yeah?"

"Look at this locker," Bonnie said.

He turned and looked at the locker the woman was filling with luggage. "So?" he said.

"What number is it?" Bonnie asked.

"It's 1563," Crew said. He turned his attention back to the baby. Then he looked at Bonnie. She was grinning at him.

"Of course," he said quietly. "Four numbers."

Crew and Bonnie both looked at the woman. She was doing her best. But it was taking her a long time. Finally, she locked the door and dropped the key into her purse. Then Crew put one of the babies into a carrier on her back. She picked up the other one and carried him in her arms.

"Thank you very much," she said.

"Don't mention it," Crew yelled over his shoulder. He and Bonnie left to find locker number 1284. They walked in front of a bench filled with people waiting for a bus.

Two of those people were waiting for something else. They had been waiting all night. They had come right from the cemetery.

Crew and Bonnie walked along the wall of lockers. "Here's 1200," Bonnie said.

"OK," Crew said. "Look down and across and we'll find it."

Bonnie stood in front of the lockers. "There it is," she said.

Suddenly, his eyes lit up. "Of course!" he said. "That's it!"

"What?" Bonnie asked. "What's it?"

"The engraving on the top of the key," Crew said. "It must have said '1284.' Whoever hid the key must have tried to scratch the number off."

"You're probably right," Bonnie said, excitedly.

"Now hurry up and open the locker."

Crew slid the key into the lock. He turned the key and the door opened.

They looked inside the locker. There was an old, yellowed newspaper. Underneath it, there was a tackle box.

"The L511," Bonnie said. "I can't believe it! We've actually found it."

Crew pulled the tackle box out of the locker.

But as he and Bonnie turned to leave with it, someone stood in their way.

"I'll take that box, folks." It was Harry.

"No," Crew said, "you don't want this box. There's a store, Nemo's, where they have a lot of these things. They would love to sell you one."

"Sorry, sport," Phil said. "We need this one."

Harry reached for the box. As he was about to grab it, Crew thrust it into Bonnie's arms.

"Run!" Crew yelled.

Bonnie held tightly to the tackle box and took off toward the bikes. Crew was right behind her. Phil and Harry raced after them.

The woman with the babies was changing a diaper on a bench. Phil didn't see a container of baby powder that the woman had left on the floor. He stepped on it and slipped, and his feet flew out from under him. Harry stopped short behind him and tried to get out of the way as Phil fell backward. But he ended up on the floor with Phil on top of him.

"You idiot!" screamed Harry. "Why don't you look where you're going!" The woman glared. The two men struggled to their feet and dashed away without stopping to apologize.

Crew put the box in Bonnie's backpack. They jumped on their bikes and took off. As they came around the front of the bus station, Phil and Harry were getting into their car.

"Follow them!" Harry screamed.

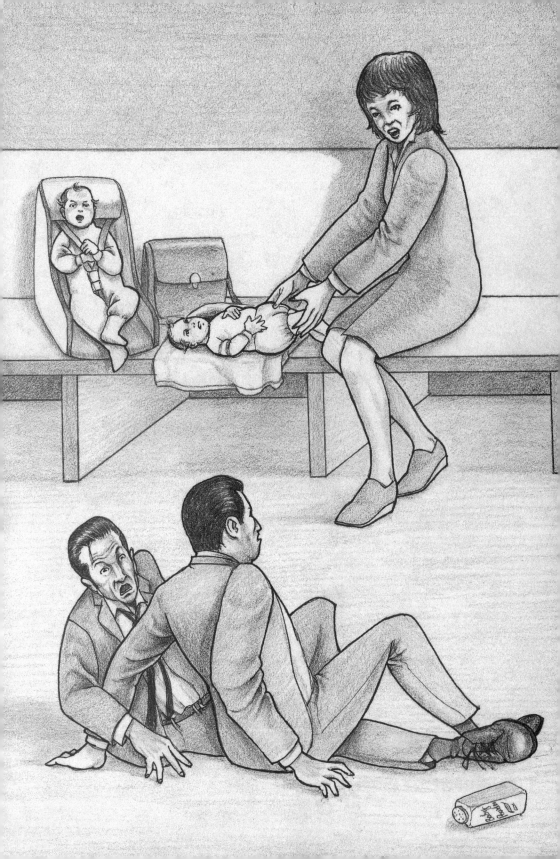

CHAPTER 7

As Crew and Bonnie rode away from the bus station, they looked back to see how close Phil and Harry were.

"They're coming after us," Bonnie yelled.

"I've got an idea," said Crew.

"I'll listen to anything," said Bonnie.

"The next cross street is Terrace Avenue," Crew said. "It's a one-way street going to our right. We can go left and ride the wrong way down the street. But they can't because they're in a car."

"Let's go," said Bonnie. They turned left onto Terrace Avenue.

When Phil and Harry got to the corner of Terrace Avenue, they saw Crew and Bonnie riding away.

"What are we going to do now?" Phil asked. "This street is one way."

"Keep going one more block on this street, to Riley Lane," Harry said. "It's one way going left."

Phil drove to Riley Lane and turned left. Now the car was moving in the direction that Crew and Bonnie were going on Terrace Avenue.

"Go a few blocks to get ahead of them," Harry said. "Then we'll swing around and meet them from the other direction."

Phil drove up four blocks and made a left onto Windsor Drive. Then he made another left onto Terrace Avenue.

"We'll get them now," Harry said. "We're heading right towards them."

Crew and Bonnie saw the car just as it turned the corner. "Follow me!" Crew yelled. He made a quick right turn onto Comet Road. Bonnie followed. Then Phil and Harry made a left turn onto the same street.

Bonnie and Crew sped two blocks up Comet Road, past Riley Lane to Pineview Drive. Bonnie's house was on Pineview. "Make a left on my street!" Bonnie said.

As soon as they turned onto Pineview Drive, Bonnie said, "Quick, go in there." She was pointing into someone's backyard. She and Crew rode into the yard.

Phil turned the car onto Pineview Drive. "They're gone!" Harry yelled. "I can't believe you lost them."

Phil said, "Hey, I'm driving. You should have been watching the kids!"

Phil stopped the car. He and Harry looked around and waited. They didn't know what else to do.

Crew and Bonnie rode through the backyards of several homes on Pineview Drive. They were headed for Bonnie's house at the end of the block. For a while it looked as if they were going to make it without being seen. But then they came to a fence. It stood between them and the last house before Bonnie's.

"I guess we'll have to get back on the street now," Bonnie said. "But if we can just get past this house, we'll be home safe."

"When we get to your house, we can call the police and get rid of those goons following us," Crew said.

They rode slowly down the driveway until they came to the sidewalk.

"I think we've shaken them," Bonnie said.

"Yeah," Crew said. "We were just too smart for them." Then he looked down the street. Phil and Harry were looking in his direction. "On

second thought," he said, "maybe not."

"Quick," Bonnie said, "my backyard!"

Crew and Bonnie practically flew into Bonnie's backyard. A few seconds later, Phil and Harry pulled up to the house.

"What do we do now?" Phil asked.

"You lunkhead," Harry said. "We go in there and get the kids and the box."

They climbed out of the car. Then they saw Crew riding out from the backyard. He was wearing Bonnie's backpack. "I'm going to the soccer field!" he yelled to her.

CHAPTER 8

"Officer," Bonnie said into the phone, "my friend is being followed by two men."

"Why is your friend being followed?" the voice asked. The officer sounded as if she didn't believe Bonnie.

"They think he has their money," Bonnie said. "But he doesn't. I do."

Bonnie had pried open the tackle box. Inside she had found stacks of one-hundred-dollar bills. Each stack was wrapped with a rubber band.

"How much money is there?" the officer asked. She sounded a bit more interested now.

"I'm not sure," Bonnie said. "It looks as if it could be $200,000."

"Give me your address," the officer said.

"My address is 11 Pineview Drive," Bonnie said quickly. "But I think my friend may be in real trouble."

"And where would he be?"

"He's at the soccer field," Bonnie said. "It's behind Edwards High School."

Crew rode onto the soccer field, and Phil drove right onto the field after him. Crew began to zigzag back and forth. Every time the car got close to him, he made a sharp turn and took off in a different direction. Then suddenly Crew's front wheel hit a rock, and he and the bike went down.

"Stop the car!" yelled Harry. Phil slammed on

the brakes, and Harry jumped out. He ran up to where Crew was struggling to get untangled from the bike. "Give me that bag," he said.

Crew was too tired to fight. He lay still while Harry pulled the backpack off his back. Phil ran up just as Harry unbuckled the bag.

"There's nothing in here but leaves!" Harry cried. He grabbed Crew's arm and yanked him up off the ground. "What gives, kid?" he snarled.

"I'm doing a science experiment for school," Crew said. "I'm trying to find out how long the average leaf can live without sunlight and water."

As Crew was talking, he heard a welcome sound: a siren.

"The cops!" Harry yelled. "Let's get out of here!"

But they weren't quite fast enough. The police car pulled up behind them. Two officers jumped out with their guns drawn.

"Freeze," one of them yelled. "Up against the car."

Phil and Harry leaned against the green car

with their legs spread. Officers frisked them and found a gun on each of them. Just then, Bonnie got out of the police car and ran up to Crew.

"Are you all right?" she asked.

Crew was clutching the backpack. "Those guys had real guns," he said. He looked a little stunned.

"Come on," Bonnie said. "We're taking you home."

CHAPTER 9

When Bonnie went downstairs the next morning, her parents were eating breakfast. There was a newspaper on the table.

"There she is," Mr. Madigan said. "The top crime-fighter in Carver City!"

Bonnie smiled. "Come on, Dad," she said. "We were just in the right place at the right time."

There was a knock on the door. "Anybody home?" Crew asked through the screen door.

"Good morning, Crew," Mrs. Madigan said. "You two should take a look at this morning's newspaper."

The headline on the paper read, "Stashed Cash Found by Teens."

"The article says the money was stolen from the Carver City Savings Bank," Mr. Madigan said. "The robbery took place five years ago."

"You mean the money was sitting in the locker for five years?" Crew asked.

"That's right," Mr. Madigan said. "Those two guys who were chasing you were working for a man named Sam Natwick. He's in prison. He's the only one who knew where the money was."

"He must have been the one sending the clues on the computer," Bonnie said.

"That's right," Mr. Madigan said. "Those two guys working for him were picking up the same clues on their computer. You two just beat them to the money."

"Well, it was a dangerous mission," Crew said. "But we pulled it off!"

Just then there was a clap of thunder. Crew looked at Bonnie. "What do you say, Bonnie?" he asked. "Do you want to go see what we can pick up on the computer?"

"I don't know," Bonnie said. "Maybe it's not such a good idea."

They looked at each other for a few seconds. Then Crew said, "I'll race you to your room."

"You're on!" Bonnie said.

They ran up the stairs to Bonnie's room.